Christmas Reflections
Forever Christmas
Book 1

Joanne Jaytanie

Look for Other books by Joanne Jaytanie
Building up to Love
Chasing Victory
Payton's Pursuit

DEDICATION
To my husband, Ralph...
For the life we have created and the Christmases we have shared.
Family is born from the heart.

ISBN-13:978-1503082526

ISBN-10:1503082520

CHAPTER ONE

"Juliet, Juliet, did you hear the news?" Annie threw the door to the clothing shop open with such force the tiny bell slammed against the wood, and made a sick tinny sound.

"It better be a fire. This is a place of business, Annie. Do not scream, or run for that matter. Mrs. Clark would have a coronary if she were here," Juliet said.

"Oh, the old bat. She needs to get a life. Maybe she should spend her days here in her shop, instead of spreading gossip."

"Gee thanks, Annie. And you call yourself my friend." Juliet giggled.

"Forget about her. Did you hear? The

Schwartz's decided to retire and their tree farm will be put up for sale."

"I heard something along those lines, but don't believe everything you hear. You and I both know the same story has fluttered through town before."

"Only this time it's true."

The shop door opened, the little bell no worse for wear. A petite blue-haired lady shuffled in.

"You're lucky you don't have to scour the town for a new bell," Juliet mumbled under her breath. "Let's finish this discussion tonight at dinner. Don't forget the wine."

****

"I can't believe they are really decided to sell," Juliet said, as she continued around the table filling her friend's wine glasses.

"They are," Adelaide said. "Barb, the mayor's assistant came in today and confirmed it. It's on tomorrow's town hall meeting agenda. Mr. and Mrs. Schwartz officially retired and are heading to the coast. They plan to buy a condo in a senior development and because none of the family wants to come back and take over the farm, it will need to be sold."

"Good for them," Lindsay said. "They are both in good health and should slow down and enjoy their golden years together." She passed the basket of bread.

"Lindsay, you are such a romantic." Juliet took the offered basket and inhaled the aroma. "This bread smells wonderful. Don't tell me you found time to bake?"

"Of course. You don't really believe I would ever bring store-bought bread to our weekly dinner?"

Juliet and her friends looked at one another and broke out in laughter.

"What?" Lindsay asked.

"Never mind," Juliet said. "Does anyone know if there is a buyer for the farm?"

"I haven't heard anyone say they want it. What happens if no one purchases it?" Adelaide asked. "I can't imagine Glenville without its Christmas tree farm. It's been part of our community for over one-hundred years. The tree farm brings a huge amount of revenue to the town."

"Someone will purchase it, eventually. The real question is who, and will they keep it a tree farm?" Juliet asked.

"What do you mean?" Annie asked. "It *is* a tree farm."

"Today. That doesn't necessarily mean a new

buyer won't have a different idea. The land alone must be worth a fortune," Juliet said.

"What would Glenville be, without its tree farm?" Lindsay asked.

"Changed," Adelaide said.

All four looked down and picked at their plates in silence.

"If I could, I'd buy the farm," Annie said.

Juliet stopped her forkful of salad in midair. "Annie, you're a genius!"

"I am?"

"She is?" Adelaide and Lindsay chimed in.

"Yes. Don't you see? For the last four years we've gotten together nearly every week and talked about how unhappy we are with our jobs and our lives are a bore. Lindsay, Adelaide, and I don't have even the slightest possibility of moving up the ladder."

"Puff...what ladder?" Adelaide asked. "But what are you implying? How can the tree farm change our jobs? I know I'm not in a position to purchase it."

Lindsay and Annie shook their heads in agreement.

"Neither am I," Juliet said. "But maybe *together*...we can."

The women stared at Juliet.

"This is what we've worked for our whole lives. I went to college and got my business degree. I've managed other people's businesses my entire career. Annie, you've got your horticulture background and own your own flower shop. Lindsay, you've been an active event planner since you started to work at the bakery. Adelaide is experienced in the import-export business. Together, we have the experience to make this tree farm a huge success."

"Let me get this straight. Four poor girls try to buy the farm? Call me crazy, but I can't see it as a selling point from the bank's point of view," Adelaide said.

"We are not poor. We each own a house and have savings."

"You really want us to take out a loan against our homes? Maybe we should think about it. I'm not sure a loan is such a great idea."

"No, not take out loans. Sell our homes."

"And what, live in a community tent?" Annie asked. "I don't know about you, but I want to spend my winter nights in a warm cozy home with walls and a fireplace."

"We will. I'm sure they will all need some work. Just the same there are five houses located on the property, a house for each of us and the main house for the tree farm."

"I can't speak for you guys, however I can't afford to have income only two months of the year. I'd need to keep my current job *and* work at the farm," Lindsay said.

"The Christmas tree income will be a good start, but the farm would stay open year 'round. We reinvent the farm into something unique, an attraction that will bring tourists and locals in 365 days a year. Each of us will remodel our own houses to include our living space and a brand new business," Juliet said. "We sell Christmas trees in the winter, and throughout the year offer nature walks, picnics, shopping, and host parties and events. Even start yearly tree planting parties."

"That sounds daunting..." Adelaide said. "And exciting. I'm in."

"Me too," echoed Lindsay and Annie.

"Okay, we go to the town meeting tomorrow and scope out the playing field. We keep this a secret, between us, agreed?"

CHAPTER TWO

Juliet, Annie, Lindsay, and Adelaide arrived early to the town hall meeting and chose seats near the back of the room, where they could get a clear view of everyone and size up any competition.

"I thought the meeting time would never get here. I've been jumpy all day," Annie said.

"You didn't tell anyone, did you?" Juliet asked, as she turned her full attention on Annie.

"*No*. I told you I wouldn't. All the same if you must know…I was tempted a few times."

All the chairs in the room filled up quickly, as townspeople continued to stream into the meeting. The volume increased each time the door opened and more of their friends and neighbors arrived.

"Where is the mayor?" Adelaide asked, as she looked at her cell phone. "This meeting was supposed to come to order five minutes ago."

"Yeah, it's not like him to be late," Lindsay said.

A few minutes later the mayor's assistant, Barb, entered from the door by the podium which lead to the adjoining courthouse. She walked up to the podium and flipped on the microphone.

"Excuse me," she said, and waited a few moments for the voices to quiet. "Excuse me, please."

"Where's the mayor, Barb?" one of the townspeople yelled. "I gotta whole barn of cows to feed. Let's get this show on the road."

"Mayor Burns got pulled into an emergency meeting about an hour ago—"

An audible groan rippled through the crowd.

"Settle down please. The mayor wanted me to give you a message. He'll be here in a few more minutes. Everyone please settle down."

"Now what?" Annie whispered.

"Don't panic, I'm sure whatever is happening has nothing to do with the tree farm," Juliet said.

"Really. And what's the likelihood our small town would experience two emergencies at the same time?"

The door beside the podium opened and Mayor Burns walked in. He looked pale and tired to Juliet, as though his world had crumbled around him, which in his case consisted of the small western Washington town of Glenville. The room instantly erupted in questions.

"Please." The mayor stretched his arms out in

front of him, and then pulled them down as if physically trying to quiet the crowd. "Everyone please stop talking." He took a sip of water and waited until a hush fell over the room. "Thank you. I'm sorry I left you all waiting, but unfortunately it proved unavoidable. There is an extremely full agenda tonight, so I suggest we get right down to it. As I'm sure you are all aware, Sam and Martha Schwartz recently made the decision to retire from their business. Much to their dismay, no one in the family wants to purchase or take over the farm. It will be put up for sale first thing tomorrow morning."

A deafening roar echoed through the hall.

"Please, one at a time," the mayor said, as he flailed his arms about.

The same farmer spoke. "I thought Sam and Martha wanted the farm to be bought by a local?"

"They would prefer to sell the farm to a local. However, they are under a time constraint and need funds to purchase their condo. They have received some interest from a corporation in eastern Washington."

"Wait one minute," Juliet said, unable to restrain herself any longer. "You told us the farm will go on the market tomorrow. How is it possible to have a potential buyer, when the farm hasn't even been listed on the open market?"

"They think a family member leaked the information. A couple other members of their family own small percentages in the farm. They of course want the farm to sell quickly and for the most money possible."

The volume in the hall crescendoed as realization dawned on the townspeople that they might lose their Christmas tree farm.

"So who has final say?" one of the townspeople yelled.

The mayor waited until everyone quieted to answer.

"Sam and Martha are the only two who can make the decisions. They are responsible for paying off their family members. They spoke to the bank and requested they be given sixty days to try and find a local buyer. After that time the farm will go up on the open market. On the bright side, it's still early in the year. The new buyer will have up to six months to ready themselves for the season, if they step up quickly and apply for the loan."

Questions and comments continued for another half hour. Finally the mayor demanded their attention.

"People, we aren't finished, there is another

issue to contend with. The reason I arrived late for this meeting is because a short while ago I received some terrible news. Glenville has suffered another blow today. It was recently discovered the business manager of the Glenville Ski Resort skimmed money for what looks like years. He fled the country last night. As you all know the owner of the resort moved away from the area years ago. He told us he'd debated selling the resort a while back, and now with this latest issue, he's no longer interested in keeping it. "

The townspeople's tempers flared with grumbles and curse words abundant. This time the mayor let them go. The crowd began to burn itself out when one of the shop owners spoke out.

"Are you telling us our town could soon find itself owned and managed by outside corporations?"

"That's the worst case scenario," Mayor Burns

said. "However, after a tense meeting with the owner's representative, they have agreed to continue to carry the note for an additional four months. As most of you are aware, the owner and his family are from the area. He attributes his initial success to the resort and would like to see it purchased by a local buyer."

CHAPTER THREE

Three months later

Juliet put the last load of glass on her work table and stretched the kinks out. Holly, Juliet's four-month-old red Doberman puppy bounded in behind her, and shook her rope tug toy.

"What do you think, Holly?"

Juliet had wanted another Doberman for years. As soon as the women learned they could purchase the farm, she called all her breeder friends to find the perfect puppy.

Holly's ears perked and she looked up when she heard her name. She dropped her toy and jumped up on Juliet's leg.

"No, you need to stay *off*," Juliet reprimanded,

and placed Holly's feet gently back on the floor as she tried not to giggle. The puppy might be cute now, but she couldn't allow Holly to jump on her customers when she was full-grown.

Juliet felt pleased with the farm's progress. In sixty short days, she and her three friends sold their houses, quit their jobs, and moved to the tree farm, which they'd renamed *Forever Christmas*. Now they worked on remodeling their new homes and shops. She looked around her shop and marveled at the change. The three outer walls now sported more windows than wood. She couldn't wait until they displayed all her stained glass pieces. Her shop was large; she had decided to use the majority of the lower floor to accommodate it. A door on the back wall led directly into her living area. Now she could walk to and from her shop without going outside. Later today her hand-carved sign would be mounted above the door and *Christmas Reflections* would officially be born.

The guys were still working on her house. She kept a small sitting area on the lower floor, with the rest of her residence on the upper level. The girls managed to employ nearly the entire town to work on their construction. As soon as all of their shops and homes were finished, the main building would be completely redone.

"I know, there are still tons left to be done, yet all in all, we've made great progress."

Holly cocked her head and yipped in response.

"Ms. Swanson!" Gina yelled as she raced into the shop.

Gina was their first official employee. She was slightly eccentric for the small town, with her short spiked hot pink hair and outlandish outfits. But she was intelligent and a quick study. Gina only recently moved from Boston to Glenville. Her family relocated four years ago, while she was in college. Gina left her posh job and moved to the town when her mom came down with mononucleosis and was having difficulty keeping up with the house and her four younger siblings.

Holly sprang up and ran to Gina. She barked and bounced around her. Gina reached down to grab her and Holly jumped back, ecstatic to play a game of keep away.

"Everyone stop!" Juliet yelled, as she grabbed a piece of glass before it vibrated off her table.

Holly and Gina froze.

"Gina, I've told you not to run into the shops. If you need to reach one of us, use the phone or if you want to come in person, walk in quietly."

"I'm sorry," Gina said. "There's a man at the

main house, named is Mr. Weatherly, and he's asking for the person in charge. Annie said you were the person to speak to."

"Of course she did."

The women discussed the division of responsibilities and she agreed to handle the day-to-day management of the farm. All major business issues would be discussed, but the rest lay squarely in her lap. She understood she was the obvious woman for the job. However, this was supposed to be a four-woman deal, Annie could just as easily have told the man they weren't yet ready for vendors.

"Well, what does he want?" She pulled her work gloves off and searched for Holly's leash.

"I asked him, and all I got from him is he wanted to speak to the person in charge."

Juliet bent down and clipped the leash onto

Holly's harness and started out of the shop. She held the door open for Gina, who got sidetracked admiring all the glittering glass.

"Wow, this glass is beautiful. What are you planning on making first?"

"I think I will start with angel tree toppers and ornaments."

"I can't wait to see them."

"Come on, let's go see what this Mr. Weatherly wants."

****

"Good afternoon, Mr. Weatherly. My name is Juliet Swanson. How may I help you?"

Colton looked up from his phone and attempted to stifle his shock. He heard the farm got purchased by a group of women, but if they were all this gorgeous, the project would be very distracting. Her straight blonde hair stopped at her shoulders, and sparkled with an array of yellow and gold. Her smile dazzled him and he found himself drawn into her eyes. He couldn't quite decide if they were blue...or grey. His daydreams came to an abrupt halt as a little red Doberman puppy barked at him. He rose to his feet and extended his hand.

"Pleased to meet you Ms. Swanson. My name is Colton, Colton Weatherly."

"We aren't open for business yet. We plan to wait until closer to the holiday season for our grand opening. I'll take your catalog and get back to you."

"Pardon?"

"Aren't you a vendor?" Juliet asked.

"No. I'm here to offer you and your friends the deal of a lifetime."

"Hmm, you sound like a salesman to me. And what might your great 'deal' be?" Juliet crossed her arms and lost her smile.

"As I'm sure you know, the neighbor to your north is the ski resort," he said.

"Yes, I'm well aware of all my neighbors. Other than my college years, I've lived here my entire life. I suppose technically the resort is our neighbor, even though it's located ten miles uphill from here."

This acquisition will be a walk in the park, with this little local girl, Colton thought. He would wrap up this deal by tomorrow evening and still make it back to Seattle in time to go to the Seahawks game.

"I didn't mean to insult you, Ms. Swanson. I represent my corporation and am in town to purchase the ski resort. We would like to make you a generous offer to acquire your little farm."

"Little farm? I assure you Mr. Weatherly, this is no such thing. For your information this farm is 100 acres, hardly what one would call *little*. We have no intention of selling to *you* or anyone."

"Please, hear me out. This is an extraordinary offer. The four of you girls can divide the money and then each start your *own* businesses."

Colton immediately realized his initial encounter wasn't going as planned. The bright red coloring he watched start at the base of Juliet's neck and work its way north was a dead giveaway.

"How dare you?" Juliet said. "This tree farm is *not* for sale. For that matter, your corporation is not eligible to purchase the ski resort. Only the townspeople from Glenville are eligible."

"You are correct. However, the current purchase restraint is only true for another thirty-seven days. On day thirty-eight, the resort will be put on the open market and my company will purchase it before the clock strikes 8:01 that very morning."

"Mr. Weatherly, I am an extremely busy woman. Feel free to finish your coffee and then kindly find your way off my property."

Juliet turned on her heels, patted her pant leg which drew her pup's' attention and headed for the door. As she turned the knob, she glanced over her shoulder and said, "Gina, please make sure Mr. Weatherly does not get *lost* on his way off the farm."

"Good afternoon, Mr. Ryan," Colton greeted his boss. He knew he pushed his luck, as he sat in his car still on the tree farm.

"Colton, tell me you have good news," Mr. Ryan said.

"I've made initial contact with Juliet Swanson, the manager of the tree farm. There's really not much more for me to do until Monday. I thought I would head home for the weekend." After he gave it some thought, Colton figured it would be best to allow Juliet the weekend to cool down.

"I hope you didn't have any big plans for the weekend. The tree farm is an extremely pivotal part of our acquisition. I want you on site until you close this deal."

"But sir, I didn't plan to stay long. I didn't bring all the project files or for that matter, my clothes."

"Fine. Head back tonight. Put everything in order at the office and pack what you need to spend the next thirty-eight days in Glenville, if necessary. I'm counting on you."

Colton stared at the disconnected phone.

Wonderful, he thought. Now he would be stuck for a month in this godforsaken backwater village. He started the car and headed for the highway. *This is going to be a long month.*

CHAPTER FOUR

"How dare he! Who does he think he is, coming on our farm and making demands?" Juliet felt so fired up when she left Colton, she almost jogged the entire way back to her shop. Holly trotted along beside her and jetted out to the end of her lead every now and then to snatch a stray branch or pinecone. Juliet sputtered and fumed the whole way.

She reached the small clearing where her shop stood and froze. Two men removed ladders from the front of her building. She gasped. A magnificent hand-carved sign painted silver and purple, adorned the space over the door: *Christmas Reflections*. Her eyes misted. Finally, her dream came true. All thoughts of Colton Weatherly evaporated from her mind.

Juliet tossed and turned in her bed. Ideas for glass patterns ran through her head. Eventually she gave up, turned on her bedroom light, threw on some sweats and a sweater, and headed for the door.

"Let's go, Holly," she said to the sleeping puppy. "There's a warm comfy bed for you in the shop."

As the first rays of morning trickled across the farm, Juliet sat back in her chair and admired the numerous patterns she'd created. Next, she would cut out the paper pattern pieces and select the glass for each piece. Lost in thought, she didn't hear the knock on her door until Holly sprang up and barked wildly. Adelaide waved a fistful of bakery bags in one hand and held a tray of coffee in the other.

"What are you doing up at this hour? Not that

I'm complaining," Juliet said, as she took the bag from Adelaide.

"I could ask you the same thing," Adelaide said, as she headed to the cupboards and grabbed plates and napkins. "By the look of things, I'd say you didn't sleep at all."

"I couldn't. I tried, but no luck."

"I hear Annie pawned some guy off on you. Gina told me what happened."

"The nerve of *Mr. Colton Weatherly,*" Juliet hissed. "I took care of him."

"You really think he'll give up that easily?"

"There's nothing left to say."

"Well, something tells me he's not done yet. Enough about Mr. Weatherly, I adore your sign. Mine is almost done. I can't wait. It's like getting the one special Christmas present I always wanted."

"So are we all going to the town picnic tonight?" Juliet asked.

"I think we should. The residents are wonderful in showing their continued support of us. We need to attend all town functions."

"All of us?"

"Yes. We are *all* going to attend the annual end-of-summer picnic."

"There's still a ton to be done. It's late September, and in a little over one month we'll celebrate our grand opening."

"I'm well aware of the timeline, Juliet. But we're business owners now, and if we expect to get support, we must show support in return. I shouldn't need to tell you of all people."

"Yes ma'am," Juliet gave her a mock salute.

"We'll pick you up at five. And don't forget to

make a dish to pass."

"Oh no. Do you think if I grovel, Lindsay would make me something sweet to take?"

"Juliet! Don't even think about it. She has her own work to do. You're a grown woman, I have faith that you can follow a simple recipe."

****

The whole town turned out for the picnic. Even the shops and restaurants closed their doors for the event. Everyone Juliet spoke with asked about the status of the tree farm. The women offered to host next year's picnic at the farm, in hopes of beginning an annual tradition.

Juliet sorted through all the luscious dishes and filled her plate, with a few extras for Holly. Holly became an instant hit with the children and Juliet allowed them to take her to play, assigning one of the older girls as leash guardian. She found the first open spot at one of the tables and sat. Before the first bite could reach her lips, a voice across the table spoke.

"Good afternoon, Ms. Swanson. I hoped I would see you here," Colton said, and smiled at her.

As Juliet looked up, she scolded herself for being so absorbed in her dinner she neglected to survey her surroundings.

"Mr. Weatherly." She tried to sound friendly yet stern. "I have to say, I'm surprised to see you at our *little* event."

He grinned and she knew he understood her meaning.

"I didn't plan to attend, someone told me if I wanted dinner this was the only place I could get it.

Now I'm glad I came."

"Why are you still in town? There's nothing to occupy your time for another thirty-six days."

"Not true. A good businessman can never gather too much information. I'm doing research."

"Uh-huh. On what?"

"The town, the people, their likes and dislikes, and the dynamics."

"Right. For some reason, I believe you're feeding me a line of bull."

He smiled a Cheshire cat smile.

She realized why she didn't instantly notice him: he fit in with his environment. Instead of the hand-tailored, exquisitely-fitting jet black suit and crisp white shirt casually opened at the neck, now he wore jeans and a button down, untucked, teal shirt. The teal intensified his whiskey-colored eyes. His onyx hair remained cut short and tight at the sides, but instead of slicked back on top, it sported a messy look, which she was sure took him a good thirty minutes to style. And his ever-present five o'clock shadow made him look sexy as all get-out.

"Ms. Swanson?"

"Hum." *Oh no.* Had she been staring? *Wonderful.* She felt her cheeks flush.

"I seem to evoke extreme emotions in you. Yesterday you were fuming and now I bore you to death."

"I'm sorry, you were saying?"

"I wondered what you do for fun on the weekends," Colton repeated.

"I work at the farm. I have way too much to do to take a weekend off. Tomorrow is a clean-up party. The entire town is invited to come out and help us clean up the farm. Afterwards we'll supply pizza and beer.

It's amazing what people will do for pizza," Juliet said.

CHAPTER FIVE

The townspeople gathered at *Forever Christmas* at eleven o'clock the next morning armed with rakes, shovels, and clippers. Juliet, Annie, Lindsay, and Adelaide, passed out large burlap bags and black trash bags. They would give all the tree limbs and clippings to the local farmers. Juliet's attention was centered on her box of bags when she heard the voice that threatened her sanity.

"Thank you," said the smooth sexy voice.

"Mr. Weatherly, what are you doing here?"

"You did say *everyone* was invited, didn't you? Besides, once again, this is the only place I can get dinner tonight. Please, call me Colton."

"Yes…I guess I did. We do have grocery stores in town. They carry food." She knew she sounded rude, so she added, "You can call me Juliet, but don't think for one minute that changes anything."

He waved his hands in submission and raised his eyebrows. "I wouldn't dream of it. Guess I just wanted some fresh air and company….Juliet." He winked.

She sighed and turned to help her girlfriends organize the crowd the watched as everyone scattered to their assigned duties.

"I hope you don't mind if I tag along," Colton said, as he jogged up beside her.

Holly roamed freely, elated with all the attention. Every now and then someone tossed her tug toy and she raced to retrieve it. Juliet smiled and then refocused her attention on the ever-persistent pushy man.

"I'd think you'd relax and enjoy your Sunday. I wouldn't think city guys like you would want to be caught dead doing this mundane work."

"Am I mistaken, or did you just insult me?" Colton asked with a smirk. "You're wrong. I spent every summer during my school years helping my granddad with his farm."

"What, too busy to help your granddad now with all your big, important business deals?"

"That has nothing to do with it. Granddad could no longer live alone and he needed to be placed in a nursing home four years ago."

"I'm so sorry." Geeze she felt like such a heel, and she was blushing—again.

"Perfectly all right, Juliet. You didn't know."

****

Colton kept an eye on her as he went about his work. He had to admit, he loved being out in the fresh country air. She was right, years had passed since he did anything physical—other than his daily gym workouts, of course. Being out among the evergreen trees doing physical labor was totally different and he wanted to soak up every minute. All too quickly he'd be back in his stuffy office, working feverishly on the next important acquisition. Still, he had the perfect life. He worked hard to get to this point, he enjoyed his life, and this was what he loved…right?

He watched Juliet flit around the tree farm, chat with everyone and still seemed to do more work than anyone else. She was a go-getter, and intelligent that one, a real firecracker. If it was any other situation,

Colton knew they would be the best of friends...or maybe more. Seemed a shame life's situations dictated one's personal decisions.

He decided he'd pushed Juliet enough today, so he took his plate of pizza and wandered over to sit under a tree. Holly joined him and he'd offered her a piece of plain crust.

"Are you still glad you came out today?" Juliet held out an icy bottle of beer to Colton and watched Holly chew up the crust.

"Thanks. I guess I should have asked you before I fed her."

"No problem. One piece is enough, though. I don't want to spend my night running outside with her if it doesn't agree with her digestive system. Mind if I sit?"

"It's your place." He winced. He needed to befriend her, not have her on edge every second they were together. "Sorry. Tired I guess. I'm not used to all this fresh air, as a city guy." *Oh, yeah. Keep it up, genius. Now you're scoring some brownie points.*

She seemed to ignore his sarcasm and sat a few feet from him. He glanced sideways at her and could have sworn she attempted to stifle a smile.

"What?" he asked.

"Just thinking. It's too bad we are on opposite sides of this fight. We seem to share some common quirks. It's a real pity."

****

Each time Juliet turned around, she expected to

see Colton lurking somewhere nearby. It surprised her that he hadn't returned to the farm since the cleanup party. She knew he was still in town, because only this morning when she went to pick up some supplies, and the coffee shop was all abuzz about Colton and his latest project: combing through the town's archives.

"What on earth could interest him in there?" Juliet asked Holly, who answered with the drop of her ball, cock of her head and a little yip. She smiled and squatted to pet her soft puppy coat. Holly rolled onto her back, and exposed her little pink belly for a rub.

Juliet stood up and refocused on her stained glass project. She created a master pattern and ran it through her oversized printer. Then she took tracing paper and carefully traced the pattern a dozen times. The trick to good fitting pieces and less glass grinding, was all in the cutting of the pattern pieces and the glass as precise as possible. The angel was a fairly simple pattern, the body in the shape of a flowing gown, with two large wings. The head was made of a round clear bevel. She planned to attach a halo made of silver wire. She would assemble these projects with copper foil and solder them together. She preferred to work with lead came and soldered joints, however smaller pieces worked better with foil. After all the pieces of the angel were soldered together, she'd cut two metal rings and attach them to the back of the angel in order to hang it to the trees.

Juliet stood up from her stool and rolled her head from shoulder to shoulder. She poured the remains of the morning coffee from the pot, rinsed it, and started a fresh pot. Holly ran circles by the door.

"Good girl. Go potty," Juliet said, and opened the shop door to let the puppy out.

The late afternoon September day was warm and sunny. She left the door open and went to fill Holly's bowl with some water. Her shop appeared to finally be coming together. She spent part of the week and unpacked all the glass creations she'd accumulated over the years. She'd designed glass for ten years and loved all her pieces. Now her designs adorned the large picture windows and filled the custom-built wood display frames. There were built-in open shelves under the windows that housed her stained glass table lamps, an assortment of candle holders, and small treasure boxes. She smiled as the multitude of colors played across the shop. It made her feel as though she was inside a child's kaleidoscope.

Bowl in hand, she walked out to bask in the warm sun. The days were just beginning to get shorter and soon would be followed by the season's first snow.

She loved the snow and could hardly wait for the first snow fall. She delighted in the thought that the grand opening of *Forever Christmas* would soon be in reach. She looked out into the trees and around her shop and then it dawned on her that she scouted the grounds for Colton.

"Forget about him. There is still much to be done before we open."

CHAPTER SIX

Colton made it his practice to know all he could about his current project and all parties involved. He'd spent the past week in exploration of the Glenville's archives. He looked at the stack of files in front of him he had yet to go though. Surprised at the amount of information the town's historian collected. "Man, don't these people believe in computers?" he asked the empty room. "It sure would go much quicker if I could look through all this information on a computer."

His cell phone rang and he frantically searched the mess of files that covered the table.

"Colton Weatherly," he clipped out, relieved he'd located the blasted thing.

"Colton, how's it coming?" Mr. Ryan asked.

"Good afternoon, Mr. Ryan. It's moving along nicely. I am in the midst of familiarizing myself with the town's history, in order to glean a better understanding of how to proceed."

"I see."

"Is there something else you would rather I work on?" Colton asked, hearing the impatience in his boss's voice.

"I assigned you to this project because you are one of my best people. Frankly, I don't give two hoots about the town's history. But if you feel the information will help close this deal, then by all means continue."

"Mr. Ryan, if you don't mind me asking, what is your long-term goal for the tree farm?"

"We will sell off the lumber to a wholesaler and break ground for condos, a strip mall, and casino in the spring. In fact, I recently received the model for the project. I'll ask my assistant to send you a few pictures. This deal will be a feather in your cap when you pull it off. I might even consider giving you a raise."

"I suppose the women could open their new businesses in town."

"I'm sure there will be a few spaces available for lease and as long as their businesses fit into the overall project, we might consider it."

"Pardon?" Now Colton was confused. His assignment consisted of securing the ski resort and tree farm. *What did the town have to do with anything?*

"My dear boy, the tree farm is merely the stepping stone for the project. After you acquire the farm and resort, we work to purchase the town itself. Our plan is to create a getaway, a place for people to go to blow off some steam and enjoy themselves. The plans for the casinos, bars, and restaurants are already drawn up. The people of Seattle will no longer have to catch a plane to spend their weekend in Las Vegas or Reno. Crystal City will be the place to go. We will provide a shuttle from Seattle to Crystal City."

"Crystal City?"

"Don't you love it?" Mr. Ryan asked excitedly. "The Board voted today on the new name. Crystal City, skiing, casinos, shows, tattoo parlors, shopping—we'll have it all! So you see, Colton, it's imperative you get this deal done on time. The farm is the kingpin to move the plan forward. All eyes are on you. Gotta go, my next client is here. Keep me updated with your progress."

Colton felt sick, which bewildered him. His company thrived on buyouts and new projects. He got assigned this project because of his ability to walk into any situation and come out on top, the hero. Why was this project different? Because up to now every other deal benefited the seller as well as his company. They were all close to, or in bankruptcy, at retirement age, or estate sales. It was a win-win. Not this time. This time his company wanted him to destroy a thriving town, full of tradition and great people. They wanted him to tear away the dream of four wonderful women. He would become the scourge of humanity to Juliet, her friends, and the entire town.

****

Colton walked Glenville's main street consumed with the conversation he'd had with his boss. Not paying attention to where he walked, he bumped into someone coming out of a store and knocked the bags from her arms. He managed to catch her before she landed on top of her bags.

"I'm terribly sorry; I wasn't paying attention. I'll take care of any damage due to my clumsiness."

"Yes you will," Juliet said, as she turned to face him.

Colton groaned. *Of all people—,* he thought to himself. "I'm sincerely sorry, Juliet, I have no excuse, I wasn't watching where I was going. How can I make it up to you?" He waited for her to tell him to take a flying leap.

"You can buy me lunch and a glass of iced tea."

"Excuse me?" he asked. Did he hear her correctly?

"I've had a busy morning. It doesn't look like yours turned out any better. I'm tired, hungry, and I need a break. Let's call a truce and enjoy one another's company over lunch. Unless you have other plans."

"Nope, no plans. I would be honored to buy you lunch. It's the least I can do." *That's an understatement*, he thought.

They walked two doors down and entered the café. Juliet sat at a table by the large picture window.

"So tell me about yourself, Juliet. You said you left town to go to school, what made you return?" Colton asked.

"This is my home. I love the comaraderie, the small town friendliness, the tradition," Juliet said and snickered.

"Why are you laughing?"

"Because all the reasons I named are the exact same reasons I left to go to California for college. I told my parents I hated living in a small town where everyone knew everyone else's business. My life plan was to get my business degree and move to a big city."

"What changed your mind?"

"The hectic pace of the city, the coldness of my neighbors, the requirement to claw your way to the top of the ladder no matter what grief you caused or whose lives you ruined, because in the city that's the only measure of success. No one knew who I really was, and no one cared. I didn't want to live my life based on their standards. I returned to the town I grew up in, where people care and they are interested in me as a person, not me as the business executive who *might* do them a favor."

"You still seem to be driven and focused. You want your farm to be a success."

"I am and I do. But on my terms."

"And your parents?"

"They are spending seven months with my older

sister and her children. Her husband is in the Navy and they are stationed in Italy. My sister is pregnant with their third child and her husband is out to sea."

"You must be lonely."

"No, but I would be if I was still in California."

"How long have your parents lived here?"

"Their entire lives. I'm the fourth generation of my family to live in Glenville. And you?"

"I grew up in Seattle, went to college at Stanford and got offered a position in Seattle right after graduation."

"Has your family always lived in Seattle?"

"My dad's family is originally from the east coast. His father bought a farm in Washington after he retired. Dad and granddad weren't what you would call close. But dad wanted to live close to his father with the hope that he could rebuild their relationship. He was offered a great opportunity with a company and travelled to Seattle in his early thirties. My mom's family moved around the state. As far as I know, they've lived in this state for generations."

"Are they both retired?"

He laughed. "My dad will never retire. His business *is* his life. I don't know what he would do without it. Mom spent her time raising us four boys. She volunteers for a variety of organizations, and when she's not busy volunteering, she hosts all my dad's events."

"Wow, four boys. I bet she had her hands full," Juliet said.

"And then some. I'm the third-born."

"What type of business does your dad own?"

"A very lucrative, very large corporation which happens to be one of my firm's major competitors."

Juliet put her glass back on the table and studied Colton. He knew exactly what she thought; he'd heard it all before. *Why don't you work for the family business? What a fool to start at the bottom when you could be at the top. Why are you building up someone else's retirement?*

"I take it you and your father don't see eye to eye."

Caught totally off guard, Colton wondered if she saw right through his façade. His father's acceptance was the one thing he'd always wanted.

"That's putting it mildly. Seems like the two of us argued since the day I came into this world. I never did anything he approved of."

"I'm sorry. Do your two older brothers work for your dad?"

"No. The oldest is a doctor, the second is a

college professor, and my younger brother doesn't possess a business bone in his body. He's a science geek. He doesn't know what he wants to do yet, except major in science. I'm the only one who ventured into the corporate world. My brothers were smart. They stayed as far away as they could, and still made my father proud. They warned me, but I never listened."

"You sound a lot alike, you and your dad. I'm sure he's very proud of you."

CHAPTER SEVEN

Colton followed Juliet back to *Forever Christmas*. He offered to help unload her car. This was his first opportunity to see her shop, and he admitted to himself, he wanted to get a look at one of the old houses. They drove past the main house that buzzed with workers, and down one of the dirt roads. Evergreen trees framed the road and blanketed the landscape as far as he could see.

She turned off the dirt road into a clearing. In the middle of the clearing, sat a pristine two-story Victorian-style house, painted in shades of lavender and trimmed with chocolate brown. The wraparound porch surrounded the house. There was a large parking area on the side of the house and at the front of the lot a large silver and purple sign read *Christmas Reflections*.

Other arrow signs in the same color scheme pointed

toward the back of the house. Colton got out of his car

and helped Juliet unload.

"Thank you again. You really didn't need to do

this. Lunch more than made up for running me over."

She grinned at him.

"My pleasure. I'm done for the day, and this

gives me the opportunity to see more of your farm. The

trees are really impressive from the road. On foot, you

don't get the same appreciation for the massiveness of

the area."

An oversized cobblestone walkway picked up at

the edge of the lot and led to the back of the house. He

turned the corner stopped, stunned by the view. The

walkway bloomed into a full patio that encompassed

the entire length of the building. The door was painted a

deep purple, and the top half featured a beautiful window made of clear leaded-glass. Above the door a large, elegantly-carved silver and purple sign read *Christmas Reflections*. Flanking the door, the bay windows burst with color, adorned with panes of stained glass in all different colors and patterns.

"You did a marvelous job, Juliet. I know a dozen people who would love to hire you, should the need ever arise." A feeling of guilt stabbed him. "How long have you done glass work?"

"Most of my adult life," she said.

"I find the name of your shop intriguing. Mind if I ask you how you decided on it?"

"It's based on my life. As we discussed over lunch, I left for bigger and better things, or so I thought. Upon reflection, I realized everything I needed to make me happy, I'd left behind."

When they entered the shop, Colton thought he couldn't be any more amazed, yet he felt as though he'd left the world behind and entered a magical land. Colors flashed and sparkled around him, rainbows danced on the shop walls. There were Christmas ornaments made from dozens of tiny pieces of glass, jewelry boxes, and glass table lamps displayed on the cherry shelves. Oversized A-frame cherry wood stands held additional framed glass windows, stunning angels with milky white wings, and holly wreaths. The Christmas tree in the corner shimmered with glass holly, santas, and snowmen. He was drawn to one of the glass table lamps.

"This is all amazing, your work is breathtaking. I love this desk lamp" he said. "Even your shelves and stands are beautiful, did you design them, too?"

"I did. A friend of mine built them. He does

wonderful work," Juliet said.

A pang of something rippled up Colton's torso, when she said 'he.' He ignored the feeling and continued.

"Can you give me his number? I would love to have some of his work for my office. This friend, are you and he close?" He practically bit his tongue, when he realized his thoughts managed to form into words.

"We've known one another since we were kids. He's the brother I never had. Let me go get Holly. She needs to go potty."

When Juliet exited the shop through a door on the back wall, Colton took the opportunity to get a closer look at the exquisite lamp. Her attention to detail floored him and her eye for color and texture was second to none.

Juliet ran back through the door, tears streaming

down her cheeks.

"Holly's missing. Someone entered through the upstairs deck and left the door ajar. Probably one of the workers—she's gone."

A ripple of fear swept though Colton and startled him.

"Did you call Gina and your three friends?"

She shook her head and tears trickled down her peach-tined cheeks.

"Here, let me make the calls," Colton said, and took the phone from her trembling hands. "Why don't you search the house and yard, maybe she's just taking a nap someplace."

He waited until she left, then he looked up the recent numbers in her phone and one by one, called them and explained the situation.

"I looked everywhere I could think of," Juliet

said, as she entered the shop.

She looked more in control but grief was visibly etched on her face.

"Annie, Adelaide, Lindsay, and Gina are all closing their shops and going out to search for Holly. Gina will round up all the workers that Holly knows and ask them to help with the search. They will all be here in a few minutes."

"It will be dark in a few hours," Juliet managed to say. "She's just a baby. She won't make it through the night. There are coyotes and bears, and it will get too cold."

"We'll find her, Juliet, don't worry. Grab a coat, some flashlights, and whatever else might help with the search."

She went to get the items and returned with a stack of tote bags. They walked outside where they were greeted by a mob of people.

"We can cover more ground if we split up," Colton said.

"Wait," Juliet said. She passed a tote bag to every other person. Each tote contained a bag of treats, one of Holly's favorite tug toys and a small flashlight. "If you see her, don't walk up on her. Squat down, talk to her in a calm soft voice and use her name. Hold the treats out at arm's length and wait for her to approach you. Otherwise you might scare her off. She's in unfamiliar territory, frightened and probably hungry. Call my mobile number if you locate her."

The crowd dispersed in every direction.

"Here." Colton handed back her phone. "Check in with me every fifteen minutes. I entered my number into your contacts. We'll find her, Juliet, I promise. I won't stop looking until we do."

He reached down, took her hand, and gave it a gentle squeeze. She smiled weakly and nodded. They split up and went in opposite directions.

Over an hour and a half passed and Colton continued to call and call for Holly until his voice turned hoarse. Every fifteen minutes, Juliet checked in with him. Each time she sounded more and more forlorn. They needed to find Holly. He knew Juliet would be devastated if she was gone forever.

He stopped and looked around him. Where would Holly wander off to? He remained quiet and listened to his environment. He thought he heard the smallest of sounds somewhere off to his right. He turned his head and listened once again...nothing...wait. There it was again. He ran full throttle off to his right. He stopped as suddenly as he started. His phone vibrated in his pocket and he reached in and pushed the off button. A tiny bark broke the silence.

"Holly?" he called in a quiet voice.

The bark sounded again and Colton walked toward the sound.

"Holly, where are you?"

A whimper came back as his answer. He walked in the direction of sound, and then stopped short at the edge of a hole. The hole wasn't deep, maybe four feet. Each time the puppy tried to climb up the steep side, she only managed to pull dirt into the hole. She was filthy and looked exhausted. She looked up at him, and panted with her mouth open and tongue out. He squatted down near the edge of the hole.

"You had us all worried sick, girl," he said, as he reached into his pocket and brought out the treats. He tossed a couple down to her and she gobbled them up. "Will you let me come down there and get you out?" She wagged her short stub and perked her ears. "We're running out of daylight. Let's get this done."

Colton sat on the edge and gingerly put his legs into the hole. Holly immediately jumped up on his legs trying to find purchase. Maybe he wouldn't need to go into the hole. He reached down and carefully placed his large hands around her exposed torso and lifted Holly up in one smooth motion. She wiggled in his grip and licked at his face to show her appreciation. Colton laughed at the puppy and held her tight against his chest with one hand as he rose from the ground. He pulled out his phone and hit the redial button.

Juliet answered on the first ring.

"Colton, what happened? Why didn't you answer my calls? I worried something happened to you too," she said.

"Call off the cavalry. I found Holly."

CHAPTER EIGHT

News of Holly's disappearance spread like wildfire through the town. People showed up to help search, while others prepared food. By the time Juliet, Colton, and Holly arrived back at her shop, picnic tables were spread out in the yard and long buffet tables overflowed with an unending variety of food and drink. Someone even put up tall posts and strung white lights around the edge of the gathering.

Holly got passed from lap to lap. Each time she'd lick the new person and then try to mooch something from the table. Juliet opened her shop and welcomed everyone in to browse. By the end of the evening, a pile of orders sat on her work table. Colton spotted them when a woman placed her order on the top of the pile. She smiled at Colton.

"Juliet does impeccable work, doesn't she?" the woman asked. "I predict by this time next year, her work will be in demand worldwide."

"Her work is incredible," he said.

Maybe they could make a go of this place, he thought. These four women were extraordinary. *Forever Christmas* meant everything to them. They would make it a success, he felt sure.

It was well after nine o'clock in the evening when the last of the townspeople left. Juliet's place looked exactly as it appeared earlier in the day, with the exception of the lights. She asked they be left up. One of the carpenters told her he would make some nice permanent posts and trade them out.

Colton was amazed at the evening's events. No

one expected anything in return. No one seemed to possess ulterior motives. They came together and did it out of caring, friendship—and community. The townspeople even welcomed him into their community, well aware of his intention to purchase the resort. How could he destroy the life these people carved out for themselves?

He stood alone on the patio while Juliet walked the last of her guests to their vehicles. Holly was in the shop, curled up on her bed snoring. It made him chuckle to hear the sound vibrate out of the small pup.

He turned as he heard Juliet approach.

"It's been a long evening. You look beat," he said to her.

She walked up to him and reached out for his hands, which took him completely by surprise.

"Thank you for rescuing Holly. I would have

been miserable if you hadn't found her." She rose up on her toes and placed a light kiss on his cheek.

For the first time in his life he found himself without words. He stared at her and soaked in her beauty. Her blonde hair glittered under the white lights and full moon. This close he could see her eyes were indeed gray-blue and hypnotizing. As if her eyes were magnets, he was drawn closer and kissed her soft, warm lips. He pulled back slightly. Then he encircled her head with his hands and drew her warmth into him. Once again he claimed her lips.

****

"Good afternoon, Ms. Swanson," Sue, the receptionist at the courthouse greeted Juliet.

"Hello, Sue. Could you tell me where Mr.

Weatherly is working today? I thought I would drag him out of here and surprise him with lunch." She held up her bags and drinks.

"Certainly. He's in the basement level, back with the archives, set up in the meeting room."

Juliet thanked Sue and headed to the stairs. She'd spent her morning in her shop and decided she needed some exercise. The three flights of stairs were a good start. She walked into the meeting room and found it empty. Files were spread over the top of the large conference table. Colton's laptop sat open in the middle of the mess. She figured he would be back in a few minutes. She set the bags and drinks on the floor and proceeded to clear a small area to put them on the table. Her eyes caught the word Glenville on the computer screen and without a second thought she read the screen.

"Glenville AKA Crystal City?" *What on earth*, she thought. She saw a brief email from his company which read, 'Attached are the pictures of our future project.' She couldn't help herself, and before she could think better of it, she clicked on the attachments. Her breath caught and her heart thumped in her throat as she stared at the future of Glenville. Where her beloved *Forever Christmas* should be, where all the sprawling evergreens should be, were condos and a casino. She started to feel light headed.

"Why, that lying—" Her throat choked with pain and anger. All this time, Colton lied to her. He pretended to enjoy the time he spent with her, when in reality he used her to collect information. What was it he said that day at the picnic? "A good businessman can never gather too much information. I'm doing research." It pierced her heart like a bolt of lightning.

She turned, ran out of the room and didn't wait for the elevator.

Juliet hurried home and packed an overnight bag and all of Holly's essentials. She'd made the mistake of trusting Colton and in return he betrayed not only her, but her entire community. How could she have judged him so incorrectly? She was a good judge of character. This time, however, seemed to be the exception to the rule.

"All you get is hurt when love is involved," she said to Holly. "You let your feelings get involved and all bets are off."

Colton lied to her. For the first time in ages she let someone into her heart and he shattered it. She could never trust him again. He may have found Holly, but was destroying Holly's home.

"If I never see him again, it will be too soon."

****

An hour later Colton walked out of the mayor's office and headed back down the stairs to the archives. As he entered the conference room, his eyes immediately tracked to the white paper bag and two drinks that sat on the table. He raced over and looked at the computer screen. He clicked the mouse to wake the screen and his blood froze as he looked at the open picture.

"No...Juliet."

He ran back down the hall and took the stairs two at a time. Sue sat at her desk and he ran over to her.

"Did you and Ms. Swanson enjoy your lunch?" she asked, before he had the chance to say a word.

"When was she here?"

"About an hour ago. I sent her down to the archives. I thought the two of you were having lunch?"

"No...no, I was in a meeting with the mayor. When did she leave?" he asked.

"I haven't seen her leave. I left my desk right after she went downstairs, and just returned."

Colton made it to the tree farm in record time. He drove directly to Juliet's shop. As he approached, he noticed her Navigator wasn't in the lot. He parked his car and ran to the back of the building. The shop was locked, but he banged on the door, and expected to hear Holly bark. He listened, but heard nothing, so he raced to the front of the house, banged on the door, and rang the doorbell. She wasn't there. *Where had she gone?* He ran back to his car and headed to the main house.

"Gina, where's Juliet?"

Gina looked up from her stack of boxes.

"Good afternoon to you, Mr. Weatherly," Gina said.

"Please, where is Juliet?"

"She left about an hour ago. She said she needed to pick up some glass."

"What time will she be back?"

"She won't be back today. She told me she'd be gone for a few days."

"Does she do this often? Where did she go? Where's Holly?"

"Holly's with her. Yes, she often goes to pick out glass and supplies. I can't tell you where for sure. She has a number of stores she visits. Can I take a message for you?"

"Just…just tell her, it isn't what she thinks."

Gina's confusion showed on her face.

Colton left the building. He got in his car, folded his hands over the steering wheel and dropped his head onto them. He knew Juliet must think the very worst of him. How could he blame her? He just came to buy the ski resort without knowing the rest of the story. Now everything had snowballed out of control, and he had needed to tell her the whole story.

Why had he thought going to work for this company was a good idea? They were known for hostile takeovers. He'd hoped he wouldn't be a lead in those deals—who was he kidding? *You idiot. And you called the Glenville residents naïve.*

He needed to explain to her. He pulled his phone out of his pocket and punched the redial button, but the call instantly went to voice mail.

"Juliet, please call me. It's not what you think, I

need to explain. Please call."

He couldn't get into the details in a message. It was too complicated and with the luck he currently possessed, she would probably take it all wrong. He wanted to stay in town and wait for her to return, but he couldn't. If he didn't leave tonight, he wouldn't be able to stop his company from moving forward with the purchase. Now all he could do was continue on with his plans and hope it all worked out. He'd come back as soon as humanly possible, and find Juliet.

CHAPTER NINE

Juliet, Annie, Lindsay, and Adelaide walked out of the town hall meeting and headed for her Navigator. Two weeks passed since Colton left town. She kept his message on her phone and played it when she wanted to hear his voice. Why did she do that to herself? No matter what he said, she knew deep in her soul he would never return to Glenville. In his heart he would always be a city guy after all and that made her heart sick with loss.

"What do you think, Juliet?" Adelaide asked.

"About what?"

"See, I told you she wasn't listening to us," Lindsay said.

"We were discussing who we thought bought the resort," Adelaide answered.

"I don't know."

"The mayor said we would know in a week or two," Annie said. "In the meantime, the grand opening will keep us busy. I can't believe it is only twenty-four short hours away. I can hardly sleep at night with all the ideas running through my mind."

"We should be getting our first snow soon," Lindsay said. "Wouldn't it be awesome if we got some in time for our opening?"

"It would be absolutely wonderful. Let's all wish upon the first star tonight. It will bring us luck," Adelaide said.

Juliet pulled into the entrance of the tree farm. Their massive sign turned out perfect. Supported between two over-sized bronze metal poles, the hand-carved masterpiece featured a background finely detailed in evergreen trees with tiny colored lights painted on them and, among the trees, sat the five houses. Along the bottom half of the sign the words *Forever Christmas* were carved and painted a metallic gold edged in red.

"He did an outstanding job on the sign," Juliet said. "I don't think I'll ever get sick of looking at it."

The door to the main house opened and Holly bounded down the stairs to greet the women.

"I made some sandwiches and brewed iced tea. I thought we could take a quick lunch before we got to work," Gina said.

The house had been restored to all its Victorian glory, with a few slight changes. The porch wrapped around from the front to the double French doors in the back. The living and dining room were now one large room. The old broken bow windows on the front wall were removed and in their place larger, energy-efficient bay windows adorned the wall of the sitting area. An antique walnut bar from a local tavern stood as the reception desk. The women designed a café which would be open for breakfast and lunch, managed by Gina and supplied by Lindsey. Gina would serve coffee, tea, hot apple cider, hot chocolate, and Lindsey's fresh baked goods for the entire day. Four large photographs were displayed in the main area, one of each of the women's shops.

The kitchen was a chef's delight. It would serve the dual purpose of daily food preparation for the café and provide food for all events. The small rooms in the back of the house were opened up and made into one large banquet room. The double French doors opened to a slate patio, which would also host events.

The upstairs of the house served as storage for the time being. They were considering creating a Bed & Breakfast by using the upstairs bedrooms.

A few of Juliet's glass pieces hung throughout the house. The scattered small side tables would host daily floral arrangements from Annie's shop. Adelaide would rotate pieces from her gift shop and they would be dispersed where shoppers could see them.

Today's task was to put up and decorate trees. They'd decided since the trees would be up all year they would bring in potted evergreens. The trees could be sold or once they grew too large for the area, they would be transplanted out in the farm.

Juliet and her friends worked non-stop through the afternoon and well into the night. Finally exhausted, they dropped into chairs and sipped on wine.

"I say we order pizza," Gina said. Juliet and the

others agreed.

"We did an awesome job, if I do say so myself,"
Annie said.

Juliet looked around the main floor. The rooms
sparkled with the feeling of Christmas.

"A job well done," she said. She and the other
women giggled well into the night as they enjoyed their
pizza and wine. Tomorrow's grand opening would be a
long day.

CHAPTER TEN

Juliet stretched and reached for her alarm. She rolled over and found Holly sitting at the side of the bed, butt wiggling.

"I know you have to go out."

Holly barked once in response and jumped up to put her front paws on the side of the bed. She licked Juliet across the cheek. Juliet giggled at her and threw back the covers.

"Are you excited Holly? I am. Today is the day. Our grand opening begins in eight short hours." Juliet opened the shade on her French door and gaped. Large white cotton puffs floated down from the sky. She threw the door open and walked out onto her deck.

Arms outstretched and face tilted skyward, she turned in slow circles while the flakes coated her face. Holly ran past her and started to snap at the snowflakes, her satiny red coat instantly covered in white. "I guess there is something to wishing on the first star," she mumbled to herself. At least one of her wishes came true.

****

"This is it," Juliet said to the women. "There's nothing left to be done, except enjoy the night."

They'd planned to start the event before dark so families could stop by with their young children. It snowed non-stop all day and the farm accumulated over nine inches of snow. A glittering white blanket covered the ground and coated the trees. The feeling of

Christmas was in the air. The wagons the horses were supposed to pull got stored away and three sleds brought out instead. Their grounds men promised to keep the roads plowed for both horses and people. All the large buffet tables in the banquet room were full of food, and champagne and wine glasses filled. With all the lights turned on, the farm sparkled like a gem. Juliet felt as giddy as a teenager; their night would be perfect.

****

The day turned to dusk as Colton approached *Forever Christmas*. Much had changed since his last visit a few long weeks ago. As he turned off the main road he was greeted with tiny white lights which lined both sides of the drive straight up to the main house. The lot overflowed with cars and people milled about.

As he parked his car he heard a whinny from a large, sleek black horse pulling a sleigh full of children and adults. The trees in the yard were dusted with white and sparkled with multicolored lights and colorful ornaments. Illuminated trees were dispersed throughout the area as far as his eye could see. The main house was ablaze, outlined with green and red lights. He could see a huge tree in the bay window, shimmering with light and color. On the top of the tree sat a glorious stained glass angel.

Colton walked up the stairs and into the house. People laughed and chatted, nearly everyone holding a plate of food or glass of champagne. He glanced at the top of the tree. Juliet's tree topper was a magnificent; he could barely keep his eyes away from it. He smiled and shook his head. The four women really pulled off a miracle.

"Hi Mr. Weatherly," Gina said, as she approached him. "I'm surprised to see you. I'm glad you could make it." She smiled up at him. "Did you see Juliet yet?"

"No. You wouldn't happen to know where she is, would you?"

"She left a few minutes ago to go to her shop. There's a buyer here from a specialty shop in Seattle. She wanted to talk to Juliet about designing some pieces for her."

He thanked Gina and headed for Juliet's shop. He couldn't find her anywhere in her shop, so he walked back outside and circled around to the front of the house. He saw her silhouette on the far side of the porch, her back to him.

"You women certainly did a spectacular job."

She whirled around. For a brief second he saw

happiness on her face, but it instantly turned to fury.

"Well, Mr. Weatherly. What are you doing here?" she asked. "Before I say something I will regret, I'll kindly ask you to leave."

He could see a sheen of tears in her eyes.

"I need you to listen to me, please—"

"There is nothing you could say that I want to hear."

"Please...let me tell you what I came here to tell you. You can throw me off your property after I finish, but please hear me out."

She studied him. *Highly likely she's weighing her options*, he thought.

"Fine. However, I want you to know there is nothing you can say to make up for what you did to my town."

"The first day I met you I told you I came here

to buy the ski resort. It was the truth. My company sent me here to secure the resort and attempt to purchase your farm along with it. I knew nothing about the takeover of the town at the time, or the fact they wanted to flatten your farm and make it into condos."

"You found out though and you didn't tell me!"

"You're right, I did and I should have told you. But you finally started to spend time with me. I wanted to get to know you and I guess I figured if I told you it would chase you off."

"And now you're here to gloat. I saw Mayor Burns tonight. He told me the resort has sold. Since it's after our deadline, I assume you completed your deal."

"I have. Just not in the way you think."

Colton watched the color drain from her face. She wrapped her arms around herself tightly and bit her lower lip. A stray tear slid unchecked down her cheek.

"Congratulations. Now please leave." She turned away.

He covered the distance between them in two strides, grabbed her shoulders and spun her back toward him.

"You said you would listen to my story. I'm not done yet."

She didn't meet his gaze. Her head hung down, but she didn't attempt to move.

"I came here thinking you were all a bunch of hillbillies and I could pull the wool over your eyes with one arm tied behind my back. I was wrong—about a lot of things. I got to know the residents of Glenville. You welcomed me from the beginning. You showed me people were capable of giving without expecting something in return, and that someone would always be there when you needed a friend. I grew to love this town, just as I grew to love you."

She looked up at him and he could see in her eyes he'd broken her heart.

"I couldn't let the corporation come in and destroy your lives and steal your town. I started digging. A good businessman—"

"Can never gather too much information. You were doing research," she frowned at him.

"Well, yes…however what I was trying to say is, with persistence you can always find a solution. I set out to find one. In doing so, I fell upon the most unbelievable piece of history. In 1903 a family named Symington owned a dairy farm at the edge of Glenville. My mother's maiden name is Symington. The day you came to the courthouse I met with Mayor Burns. I told him what I found out, made him promise not to breathe a word of it to anyone. I told him with luck I could save the resort."

"Wait…are you trying to tell me your mom's family is from Glenville?"

"I wasn't positive. When I couldn't find you I made the difficult decision to return to Seattle. The Symingtons were my mother's great grandparents."

"Even so, I can't believe she would want to buy the resort."

"She doesn't want the town her family came from to disappear, before she even gets the chance to see it."

"I can't believe you have the money to purchase the resort."

"I don't, my father does."

"Your father and you don't see eye to eye when it comes to business. Why would he even think of helping?"

"He and I had a long heart-to-heart talk. I realized a great deal about myself during my time here. Turns out my father and I are much alike. I took the job with the competitor to tick him off, to show him I could stand on my own, and make my own way without his help. Truth be told, I've really missed him over the past few years. We've spent holidays together, but I never went out of my way to talk to him. He told me he understood I needed to do what I needed to do. He did the same thing when he left his dad's business to strike out on his own. It took him over thirty years to rebuild his relationship with his dad and he didn't want the same thing to happen to us."

"He purchased the ski resort?"

"No, he couldn't. He's not direct bloodline to anyone here, I am. We formed a partnership, put my mom on the board of directors and I purchased the resort."

"And now you can go back home with your first big deal in the bag," Juliet said. He could tell she still didn't believe he was there to stay.

"That's just it. I am home. I want to live in Glenville and grow old in Glenville. I'm hoping you will give me a second chance. I promise I will never break your heart again.

****

The ski resort was closed while Colton did a complete remodel with plans for the grand opening on New Year's Day. He spent every day at the ski resort from morning to night getting it ready for the season. Now he sat on the sofa with his computer open and Holly next to him curled into a tight ball, her nose tucked under her leg.

Juliet carefully placed the stained glass angel on the top of the tree. Christmas Eve crept up on them and this was the first chance they had to decorate her tree. After the grand opening orders poured in, she had no time to do any of her own decorating.

"Put that thing away now. Let's enjoy the holiday. This is the only time we will celebrate the first Christmas at the farm," she said.

"I will. Come here first. I want to show you a picture of the ski resort's new sign."

She disappeared behind the tree and returned holding a large wrapped gift. She placed it gently on the coffee table and dropped down beside him. "First I want you to open this gift."

He set his computer aside and opened the gift. Inside he found the table lamp he had adored the first day he walked into her shop.

"I thought you had sold it," he said with surprise.

"That's what I wanted you to think," she said with a giggle.

"I love it. Thank you. It will go in my office, where I can look at it every day."

"Did you finally decide on your new catchphrase?" she asked him, as he put his arm around her.

"Yes, the perfect one," he said with a smile. He pushed a key on the computer and turned the screen toward her.

Juliet read it aloud. "Glenville Ski Resort…Come Home Again." The sign was beautifully carved. "It's beautiful."

"So are you," he said. He turned her toward him

and kissed her.

Holly jumped down, pushed her way between them and poked at them with her wet nose. They both laughed as she smiled at them.

"Holly, you've kept your ribbon on today." In the holiday spirit, Juliet tied a new ribbon around Holly's neck each day. "You look good in purple and silver." She rubbed Holly's cheek, then straightened the ribbon and her finger touched something metal. "What—?" She dug though the bow and found a dazzling emerald-cut diamond ring. "It's gorgeous, Colton."

"Merry Christmas, sweetheart." Colton said. "Let's make this Christmas the first of our family traditions."

LOOK FOR THE OTHER THREE

BOOKS

IN THE SERIES
FOREVER CHRISTMAS

The western Washington town of Glenville is threatened with the possible loss of their 100 year old Christmas tree farm to an outside corporation.

Four friends join together to keep the tradition alive and create new opportunities with the rebirth of, Forever Christmas tree farm.

CHRISTMAS KISS
SHARON KLEVE

Adelaide Duval has been told how to live her life from a very early age. First by her mother and then by her jerk boyfriend Jason. Both leave her expectantly and now she's starting over with a new home and a new business. A new romance never crosses her mind.

Roman Bennett leaves his old life behind in the big city and settles into the small town of Glenville. When he meets Adelaide, his wounded heart is healed with a Christmas Kiss.

THE CHRISTMAS WREATH

ANGELA FORD

Annie Dixon's love for nature and her hometown of Glenville has her driven to find a way to keep the tree farm from outsiders. When the bank grants sixty days before the tree farm is listed for public sale, Annie and her friends devise a plan to finance the buy.

The death of Annie's childhood friend brings Detective Ryder Harris back to Glenville. A child in his eyes, he always called her 'Sweet Annie'. Now he sees her differently. Annie never admitted she had a big crush for Ryder. Now that familiar flutter in her heart is back. Annie knows Ryder won't settle in Glenville. And is Ryder really back for his sister's funeral or is he connected to the town resort's sudden disappearance of their manager?

For the first time in many years, Ryder is excited about the holidays. Will the magic of Christmas forever connect these two hearts?

CANDY CANE KISSES

ELLE RUSH

All bakery-owner Lindsay Leeds wants for Christmas is for her former high-school crush Sheriff Keith "Bodey" Bodewell to quit playing games. The sheriff has been dancing around asking her out for months and Lindsay is tired of it. His "fake girlfriend" ploy was cute and it was sweet that he recruited her friends to find out what she likes, but enough is enough. She's a busy woman and he needs to step up or he's going to lose his shot.

How can a woman who runs two businesses be so clueless when it comes to managing her heart? Bodey has dropped more than enough hints that he's interested, but Lindsay isn't catching them. Just when the sheriff is running out of ideas on how he can convince her to be his for Christmas, Lindsay gives him a clue about what it will take for him to get a date. And the answer is pretty simple. At least, it was supposed to be. Christmas is days away and his plays keep failing on a spectacular level.

It's going to take the jolly fat man to make this holiday romance happen.

ABOUT THE AUTHOR
JOANNE JAYTANIE

Joanne was born and raised in Sherburne, New York, a quaint village surrounded by dairy farms and rolling hills. From the moment she could read she wanted to explore the world. During her college years she slowly crept across the country, stopping along the way in Oklahoma, California, and finally Washington State, which she now proudly calls home. She lives with her husband and Dobermans, in their home located on the Kitsap Peninsula with a panoramic view of the Olympic Mountains.

Joanne writes paranormal, romantic suspense. She loves writing about the twists and turns of her character's lives and the trouble they find themselves involved in, coupled with building an everlasting relationship. She is a member of Romance Writers of America, and an active member of Debbie Macomber's home chapter, Peninsula Romance Writers, where she currently serves as the President.

Made in the USA
Charleston, SC
11 November 2016